GEORGE ELLA LYON and PETER CATALANOTTO

a richard jackson book   atheneum books for young readers   NEW YORK   LONDON   TORONTO   SYDNEY

No dessert forever!

For my cousin Susan, who said it,
and for all the Littles and Bigs who hold this book

—G. E. L.

For Debbie and Betsy,
with tremendous appreciation for all you do

Special thanks to Grace and Jake

—P. C.

Atheneum Books for Young Readers
An imprint of Simon & Schuster Children's Publishing Division
1230 Avenue of the Americas
New York, New York 10020
Text copyright © 2006 by George Ella Lyon
Illustrations copyright © 2006 by Peter Catalanotto
All rights reserved, including the right of reproduction in whole or in part in any form.
Book design by Ann Bobco
The text for this book is set in Imperfect.
The illustrations for this book are rendered in watercolor and gouache.
Manufactured in China
First Edition
2 4 6 8 10 9 7 5 3 1
CIP data for this book is available from the Library of Congress.
ISBN-13: 978-1-4169-0385-7
ISBN-10: 1-4169-0385-2